STAR WARS

EPISODE I 3D
THE PHANTOM MENACE

By Pablo Hidalgo
Based on the story and screenplay by George Lucas

SCHOLASTIC INC.

New York • Toronto • London • Auckland • Sydney • Mexico City • New Delhi • Hong Kong

www.starwars.com

SCHOLASTIC
www.scholastic.com

Copyright © 2012 Lucasfilm. Ltd. ® & ™ where indicated.

All Rights Reserved. Used Under Authorization.

Published by Scholastic Inc., 557 Broadway, New York, NY 10012
Scholastic and associated logos are trademarks of Scholastic Inc. No part of this book may be reproduced, stored in a retrieval system, or transmitted in any form or by any means, electronic, mechanical, photocopying, recording, or otherwise, without the prior permission of Scholastic Inc.

Produced by becker&mayer!, LLC.
11120 NE 33rd Place, Suite 101
Bellevue, WA 98004
www.beckermayer.com

If you have questions or comments about this product, please visit
www.beckermayer.com/customerservice.html and click on the Customer Service Request Form.

Written by Pablo Hidalgo
Edited by Delia Greve
Designed by Rosanna Brockley
Design assistance by Cortny Helmick
Photo research by Katie del Rosario
Production management by Jennifer Marx
3D anaglyph conversion by Richard Anderson, Matthew Fisher, Cortny Helmick, Joe Mentele, Brandon Walker, and Bill Whitaker

Special thanks to Carol Roeder, J.W. Rinzler, Troy Alders, and Leland Chee at LucasBooks

Printed, manufactured, and assembled in Dongguan, China 8/11.

10 9 8 7 6 5 4 3 2 1

ISBN 978-0-545-38986-0

11699

For generations, the galaxy has been peacefully governed by the Galactic Republic and protected by the Jedi Knights. The corrupt Trade Federation has grown powerful and rich by controlling shipments of supplies between planets. When the Republic tries to collect its share of the profits, the greedy trade barons threaten the peaceful world of Naboo.

Viceroy Nute Gunray, leader of the Federation, surrounds Naboo with warships and cuts off trade to the planet. In response to this bold move, the Republic dispatches two ambassadors to resolve the dispute.

The Ambassador's cruiser lands in the Trade Federation flagship hangar, which is patrolled by battle droids. These robotic soldiers obediently carry out the orders of the Trade Federation.

No living being greets the ambassadors. Instead, a protocol droid ushers them into an empty conference room. The diplomats are Jedi Knights who wield the mystical power of the Force. Jedi Master Qui-Gon Jinn and his apprentice, Obi-Wan Kenobi, wait for negotiations to begin.

On the battleship's bridge, Viceroy Gunray receives transmitted orders from his mysterious master, Darth Sidious. When informed about the Jedi diplomats, Sidious snarls, "Kill them immediately." As a Sith Lord, **Sidious longs to rid the galaxy of all Jedi Knights**.

Meanwhile, in the hangar, a laser cannon blows apart the Jedi's cruiser. **Qui-Gon and Obi-Wan sense through the Force that they are in danger.** The two Jedi Knights spring from their seats, igniting their lightsabers as air vents begin spouting deadly gas into the conference room! "Dioxis!" says Qui-Gon, before holding his breath.

Convinced the Jedi must be dead, a squad of battle droids opens the conference room. **Obi-Wan and Qui-Gon leap into the corridor, slashing through the droids with their lightsabers.** Watching via security cameras, the Neimoidians panic. "I want droidekas up here at once!" Gunray shouts. Destroyer droids roll into action and unfurl, revealing heavy laser cannons and defensive shields.

Qui-Gon and Obi-Wan retreat into the battleship's ventilation shaft and emerge in a hidden hangar bay where thousands of battle droids are readying landing craft and assault vehicles. "It's an invasion army," remarks Obi-Wan.

"We've got to warn the Naboo," Qui-Gon replies. "Stow aboard separate ships and meet down on the planet."

On Naboo, the government fears a battle with the Trade Federation army. **"I will not condone a course of action that will lead us to war,"** says Queen Amidala, the planet's 14-year-old ruler. She has faith that Naboo's galactic representative, Senator Palpatine, can find a peaceful solution from Coruscant, the Republic capital.

The Trade Federation invasion begins. Landing craft descend into the planet's swamps, unloading battle droids and heavily armored transports.

The tanks push their way through the swamps, toppling trees and crushing shrubs. Terrified animals gallop, slither, fly, and skitter away from the intruders.

The Jedi Knights run alongside the wildlife. In dodging a troop transport, Qui-Gon runs smack into a shrieking swamp-dweller. "Oh, nooooo! Aye-yai-yeeee!" screeches the rubbery-limbed being, as he clings to the Jedi for protection. **Jar Jar Binks is a native amphibious Gungan who lives in the Naboo swamps.**

"Oh, mooie-mooie! I love you!" gushes Jar Jar, pledging his devotion to Qui-Gon for saving his life. Jar Jar helps the Jedi by leading them to the Gungans' hidden city of Otoh Gunga. "Wesa goin underwater, okiday?" Jar Jar asks as he dives into a lake. The Jedi have no choice but to follow him.

Jar Jar isn't welcome in Otoh Gunga—he was banished for his clumsiness by the Gungan leader, Boss Nass. **Nass doesn't like outsiders or the Naboo surface-dwellers.** "Day tink day brains so big," he complains. Using the Force, Qui-Gon persuades Nass to lend him a transport, called a bongo, so he can warn the Naboo of the invasion.

To reach the Naboo, the Jedi must go through the planet core. While the Gungans' unique underwater atmosphere bubbles keep Qui-Gon, Obi-Wan, and Jar Jar dry—there are more dangers deep in the underwater caves. "Goen through da planet core? Bad bombin'," says Jar Jar.

As the bongo travels deeper, the tiny submarine attracts the attention of an enormous opee sea killer. It snatches the bongo with its long, sticky tongue. But an even larger creature—the sando aqua monster—chomps down on the opee, causing it to release the bongo! **"There's always a bigger fish,"** observes Qui-Gon wisely.

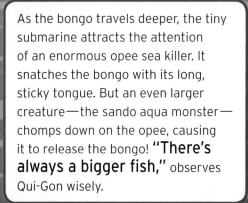

To escape, the damaged bongo races into a cave and runs into an even bigger fish—a fanged colo clawfish! Jar Jar begins to panic. The still-hungry sando monster once again comes to the rescue, grabbing the clawfish and allowing the bongo to get away.

In Theed, the Naboo capital, battle droids march down the vine-laced avenues and round up citizens as a captive Queen Amidala watches sadly. Viceroy Gunray emerges from a shuttle, relishing his conquest. "Ah, victory!" he says, beaming.

Battle droids surround Queen Amidala, her advisers, and her royal handmaidens. In addition to tending to her royal gowns and elaborate hairstyles, each handmaiden is a trained bodyguard for the Queen.

As the droids march the captives past an overhead walkway, the Jedi leap down with their lightsabers drawn. **With a flash of their blades, Qui-Gon and Obi-Wan turn the droids into scattered fragments!** "We should leave the streets, Your Highness," advises Qui-Gon. The Jedi plan to escort Amidala to Coruscant, where she can plead for help from the Senate.

In the royal hangar, a squad of battle droids guards the Queen's starship and holds its crew prisoner. "I'm taking these people to Coruscant," says Qui-Gon as he calmly walks up to the droids. When the confused droids refuse to comply, Qui-Gon and Obi-Wan destroy them with their lightsabers.

The royal starship blasts into the Naboo skies. "There's the blockade!" shouts the Queen's pilot, Ric Olié, as he points the vessel toward the ring of Trade Federation battleships. Heavy laser cannonfire erupts all around the Naboo vessel.

"The shield generator's been hit!" cries Olié, as the Naboo starship's deflectors shut down. Emergency astromech droids roll onto the ship's gleaming surface to repair the damage. Enemy fire begins knocking them off one by one.

One droid, R2-D2, bravely sticks with the repairs and resurrects the ship's shields. The royal starship blasts into hyperspace. The droid returns to safety inside, where Queen Amidala commends his devotion. "Thank you, Artoo-Deetoo," she says.

"It's impossible to locate the ship!" stammers Gunray as he skittishly reports to Sidious that the Queen has escaped.

Sidious is not so easily defeated. **"This is my apprentice, Darth Maul. He will find your lost ship,"** Sidious says.

The damage to the royal starship's hyperdrive limits its range. Unable to make it all the way to Coruscant, the ship sets down on nearby Tatooine for repairs. "It's small, out of the way, poor," says Obi-Wan, describing the desert planet that is controlled by Hutt gangsters.

Qui-Gon Jinn, dressed as a local peasant, leads R2-D2 and Jar Jar Binks into the town of Mos Espa to find a replacement hyperdrive. "The sun doen murder to mesa skin," gripes the Gungan. The Queen is curious about the planet and sends along her handmaiden Padmé.

In Mos Espa, **they find a junk shop filled with droids, Podracer engines, and starship parts.** The fluttering Toydarian junk dealer, Watto, sees a chance to make some money. "Let me take thee out back, huh? You'll find what you need," he says.

In the shop, Padmé meets Anakin Skywalker—a 9-year-old mechanic, pilot, and slave owned by Watto. **Anakin tells Padmé she is one of the most beautiful people he has ever seen.** "You're a funny little boy," Padmé says, charmed.

Watto has a hyperdrive generator, but Qui-Gon can't pay for it. "Republic credits are no good out here," explains Watto. "I need something more real." **Qui-Gon can't even use the Force to change Watto's mind.** "What, you think you're some kind of Jedi, waving your hand around like that?" Watto says. "I'm a Toydarian. Mind tricks donna work ona me—only money."

Qui-Gon, Padmé, Jar Jar, and R2-D2 return to the Mos Espa streets empty-handed. As they walk past a food stand selling juicy frogs, Jar Jar's hunger gets the better of him. He can't help but try to nab one with his long tongue. Instead, **Jar Jar sends the frog flying**!

The frog lands in Sebulba's bowl of soup. The ill-tempered Dug may be short, but his fists are big. **The local thug pounces on Jar Jar, ready to pound him.** But when Anakin appears, he warns Sebulba to stay away from his newfound friends.

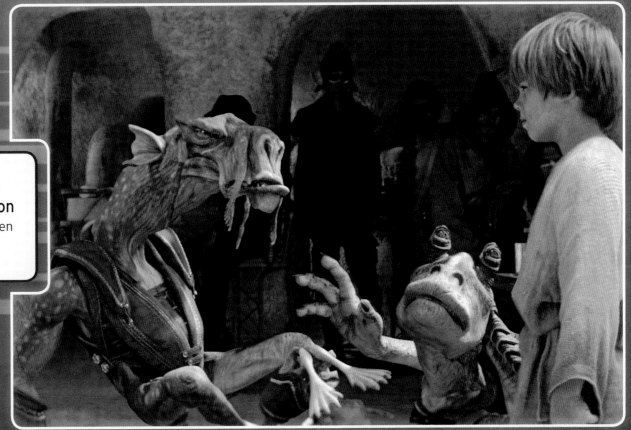

"Thanks, my young friend," Qui-Gon says to Anakin. The boy leads them to a less dangerous food stand. As Qui-Gon picks out some food, Anakin spots a lightsaber hidden beneath Qui-Gon's robes and realizes the stranger must be a Jedi Knight! **Anakin dreams of one day becoming a Jedi.**

A sandstorm approaches Mos Espa. It's too late for Qui-Gon, Jar Jar, and Padmé to get back to their ship. "Sandstorms are very, very dangerous," warns Anakin. "Come on. I'll take you to my place." He leads them to the slave quarters he shares with his mother, Shmi Skywalker.

"Your son was kind enough to offer us shelter," Qui-Gon explains to Shmi. Her son is often full of surprises, so four sudden guests hardly faze Shmi.

"Come on, I'll show you Threepio!" says Anakin, hoping to impress Padmé. **C-3PO is a protocol droid Anakin has cobbled together to help his mother.** R2-D2 points out the droid is missing his coverings.

"My parts are showing!" cries an embarrassed C-3PO. "My goodness! Oh!"

Over dinner, Qui-Gon reveals that they are on a vital Jedi mission to Coruscant, but they are stranded on Tatooine until they can repair their ship. Anakin suggests he can earn the needed parts with his astonishing Podracing skills. **"I'm the only human who can do it!"** he boasts.

The next day, Qui-Gon begins putting Anakin's plan into action. He bets the Queen's ship against Watto's spare parts in the upcoming Podrace, certain that Anakin will win. The offer is irresistible to the greedy Watto. "Your friend is a foolish one, methinks," he tells Anakin.

Later, Qui-Gon and Shmi watch as Anakin prepares his Podracer. **"The Force is unusually strong with him,"** says Qui-Gon.

Shmi reveals that Anakin has no father. "I carried him. I gave birth. I raised him," she says. "I can't explain what happened." Anakin may have been brought to life through the will of the Force.

The mechanics of a Podracer seem simple—energy binders hold together rocket engines tethered to a cockpit or pod—but it takes technical precision to make one a champion. Anakin is certain that his is the fastest ever built. Everyone works together to put the finishing touches on the Podracer.

Even Jar Jar lends a hand, though he does accidentally get his tongue caught in the energy binders. The electric jolt zaps Jar Jar's mouth numb.

Later that night, Qui-Gon cleans a scrape on Anakin's arm and takes a sample of the boy's blood. He transmits it to Obi-Wan on the Queen's ship for analysis. Anakin has over 20,000 midi-chlorians in his blood sample—**he has more Force-potential than any known Jedi.**

Meanwhile, elsewhere on the planet, the Sith Infiltrator cuts through space and lands in the predawn darkness not far from Mos Espa. Its hatch opens, and Darth Maul, the fearsome apprentice to Darth Sidious, emerges.

His tenacious tracking skills have led Darth Maul to the planet where the Queen is hiding. **Maul longs to strike against the Jedi.** He summons a trio of probe droids—hovering spheres, packed with sophisticated sensors—to search the desert town for the fugitives.

The next morning, Qui-Gon proposes an additional bet to Watto. If Anakin wins the race, Watto will set him free. If Anakin loses, Qui-Gon will give the Podracer to Watto. Watto agrees to the wager, because he is betting on Sebulba. "He always wins!" Watto crows confidently.

It's Boonta Eve—a Hutt holiday celebrated with the classic Podracing challenge. **Tens of thousands of spectators fill the Mos Espa Grand Arena to watch and bet on the race.** The event is hosted by the loathsome gangster Jabba the Hutt.

To be an effective Podracer pilot, you need as many advantages as possible. Almost all of the eighteen pilots are aliens gifted with special senses, extra eyes, lightning reflexes, or extra arms that give them a racing edge. Some Podracers are huge and rely on engine power, while others are sleek and have excellent maneuverability.

The three-eyed Mawhonic from Hok, the scrappy little Ratts Tyerell from Aleen, and the flamboyant Teemto Pagalies of Moonus Mandel are among the competitors. But the crowds cheer loudest for Sebulba, and the Dug basks in the adoration of the audience. **Sebulba's Podracer is customized with a variety of hidden—and illegal—weapons to take out other racers and ensure his own victory.**

"**Begin the race,**" Jabba the Hutt orders. The Podracers roar to life, but Anakin's engines immediately flood.

"Oh, no!" cries Anakin. He quickly restarts his thrusters and joins the race.

"He will be hard-pressed to catch up with the leaders!" the Podrace announcers predict.

Sebulba immediately shows his true colors by slamming his Podracer into his nearest competitor. Mawhonic's Podracer crashes into the mighty stone monuments of the Mushroom Mesa.

Podracers squeeze through the stone wickets of Arch Canyon, jockeying to lead the way through the narrow obstacles.

As if the natural terrain isn't dangerous enough, the pilots must avoid shots from Tusken Raider snipers who are camped out on the Canyon Dune Turn.

Anakin quickly makes up for his late start by weaving past Teemto Pagalies and Gasgano in the second lap.

Sebulba keeps up his dirty tricks and tosses a piece of scrap into Mars Guo's massive Podracer engines. The engines explode, littering the racecourse with scraps of metal.

A piece of Guo's broken Podracer slices through Anakin's control tethers. "Skywalker's spinning out of control!" the announcers shout. Anakin uses a special tool to grasp his flailing tether and snap it back into place.

"At the start of the third and final lap, Sebulba's in the lead, followed closely by Skywalker!" the announcers call out. Sebulba constantly shifts his position on the raceaway to keep Anakin from sneaking past.

The Dug forces Anakin to veer onto a service ramp. Anakin's Podracer flies high into the air. But Sebulba's trick backfires. Anakin soars past Sebulba and drops his Podracer into the lead.

Sebulba accelerates, his loud engines hovering less than a meter behind Anakin. One of Anakin's thrusters begins to overheat. He quickly redistributes power, but Sebulba pulls ahead.

The two Podracers are neck-and-neck. Sebulba tries to knock Anakin off course but accidentally locks their Pods together! **Anakin pulls free, causing Sebulba to spin out.** His massive thrusters slam into a rock, and his cockpit hits the ground.

Anakin zips ahead and crosses the finish line first. The crowd erupts in cheers. "Mom, I did it!" cries Anakin.

Shmi is relieved her son survived the treacherous race. "It's so wonderful, Ani," she says. "**You've brought hope to those who have none.** I'm so very proud of you."

Watto bet everything on Sebulba, and now he is ruined. He is livid as Qui-Gon arrives to collect his winnings. "You! You swindled me! You knew the boy was going to win. Somehow you knew it!"

Qui-Gon hauls the new hyperdrive generator to the Queen's ship. Obi-Wan is relieved that his Master's risky plan worked. Qui-Gon then returns to town, where he plans to take Anakin with him, away from Tatooine.

Although it breaks her heart to say good-bye to her son, Shmi knows Anakin could become a great Jedi Knight. "Now you can make your dreams come true, Ani," she says. "You're free."

With great difficulty, Anakin leaves his mother behind. **"I will come back and free you, Mom,"** he vows.

One of Darth Maul's probe droids spots Qui-Gon and Anakin returning to the Queen's ship and reports back. Darth Maul mounts his Sith speeder and rockets into the desert. The time to attack has come.

Qui-Gon spies the dark warrior approaching. **"Anakin, drop!"** he shouts. The boy dives to the sand just as the Sith speeder soars over him. Maul leaps at Qui-Gon, igniting his weapon in midair. For the first time in centuries, **Sith and Jedi lightsabers cross**.

Qui-Gon is stunned by the dark warrior's speed and skill. **Maul keeps hammering at Qui-Gon with his red-bladed lightsaber**, trying to cut through the Jedi Master's defensive parries. Anakin runs ahead to the Queen's starship.

The Queen's ship takes off and flies past the lightsaber duel. Qui-Gon leaps high onto its open entry ramp. The Jedi escapes! Maul watches from below as the silver ship disappears into the sky.

Qui-Gon is exhausted after fighting such an intense opponent. **"It was well trained in the Jedi arts,"** he tells Obi-Wan. Have the Sith somehow returned after a thousand years? It is a matter to be discussed with the Jedi Council—as is Anakin's remarkable Force potential. They must be patient. "Anakin Skywalker, meet Obi-Wan Kenobi," says Qui-Gon.

Anakin has never been aboard a starship. It's cold in space. He shivers in the dark, missing his mother. Padmé places a blanket over him. Anakin gives her a gift: an amulet he made. "I carved it out of a jappor snippet," he says. "It'll bring you good fortune."

The Naboo starship arrives on Coruscant. Anakin has never seen anything like the Republic capital. **"The whole planet is one big city,"** explains Ric Olié. The starship lands on a floating platform, where the Queen is greeted by representatives from the Senate.

Amidala and Senator Palpatine stand in the Naboo delegation pod in the massive Senate chambers. Amidala pleads for the Republic to help her planet, but instead the Senators bicker over proper procedures. Disgusted, and at the urging of Senator Palpatine, Amidala calls for a change in government leadership.

There is an immediate election to name a new supreme chancellor. Senator Palpatine is in the running. "I feel confident our situation will create a strong sympathy vote for us," he tells Amidala. But her faith in the government is shaken. She wants to go home to help her people. Jar Jar is homesick, too.

Meanwhile, Qui-Gon reports his suspicions about his attacker to the Jedi Council. He also requests for Anakin to be tested to become a Jedi, even though the boy is older than Jedi typically are when they begin training. **"He will become a Jedi,"** Qui-Gon tells Obi-Wan. Obi-Wan urges his Master to not defy the Council. "I shall do what I must, Obi-Wan," Qui-Gon responds.

The Council examines Anakin and tests how keenly he can perceive things through the Force. He is indeed gifted, but Masters Yoda and Mace Windu are concerned. **"I sense much fear in you,"** says Yoda. Anakin is afraid he'll never see his mother again.

"He will not be trained," Mace Windu informs Qui-Gon.

"Clouded this boy's future is," adds Yoda. Qui-Gon disagrees. **He believes Anakin is the Chosen One of an ancient Jedi prophecy—the one who is destined to bring balance to the Force.**

"The boy is dangerous," Obi-Wan warns Qui-Gon.

"His fate is uncertain," Qui-Gon says. "He's not dangerous." Although Qui-Gon is forbidden to train Anakin, he continues to look out for the boy. "Always remember: Your focus determines your reality," Qui-Gon tells Anakin. "Stay close to me, and you'll be safe."

The Queen returns to Naboo with only a small crew and the Jedi Knights to protect her. There is no way for her to defeat the Trade Federation blockade without an army. But Amidala has a plan. "Jar Jar Binks," she calls. "I need your help."

Jar Jar informs Amidala of the Gungan Grand Army. The Gungans are a proud people with a warrior tradition, and they too have been affected by the invasion. The Queen's ship lands in the swamps of Naboo. Its crew treks to the secret, sacred place where the Gungans have taken refuge.

Amidala asks the Gungan leader, Boss Nass, for help. But Nass thinks all Naboo are too big-headed and arrogant to ever see eye-to-eye with his people. But then Padmé steps forward and reveals she is the real Queen! The other is her bodyguard. Padmé kneels before Nass and pleads for his help. Nass reconsiders when he sees this. **"Maybe wesa bein' friends,"** he says with a huge grin.

Amidala's return and the gathering Gungan army make Nute Gunray increasingly nervous. At the captured palace in Theed, Gunray consults with Darth Sidious via hologram. Sidious is surprised by Queen Amidala's boldness and orders Gunray to attack. **"Wipe them out,"** he says. **"All of them."**

Amidala, Boss Nass, and their advisers plot their attack. The Gungan army will draw the droid forces out of the city and into the plains. This diversion will allow Amidala and her troops to infiltrate Theed, capture Gunray, and launch a squadron of starfighters to take down the orbiting Droid Control Ship that commands the droid army.

The mists of the swamps part as thousands of Gungan soldiers march overland. Jar Jar Binks leads the army. In gratitude for his service, Boss Nass promoted Binks to general.

"Starten up da shields!" a Gungan officer calls. Generators, carried on the backs of huge faamba creatures, create an umbrella of shield energy over the Gungan army. The shimmering barrier protects the Gungans from droid blasters and artillery, although slow-moving objects can pass through.

While the Gungans prepare for battle, Amidala and her troops sneak into Theed. Naboo soldiers open fire on the droid patrols, sparking a fast yet decisive battle. Amidala dodges incoming blaster bolts, flanked by Qui-Gon Jinn and Obi-Wan Kenobi, who protect her with lightsabers.

The Queen's troops blast the droids standing guard in the royal hangar. "Ani, find cover!" Qui-Gon orders. Anakin scurries to get out of the way.

"Get to your ships!" Amidala commands her pilots. They run to the awaiting Naboo starfighters. The sleek yellow vessels soar out of the hangar and into the blue skies above.

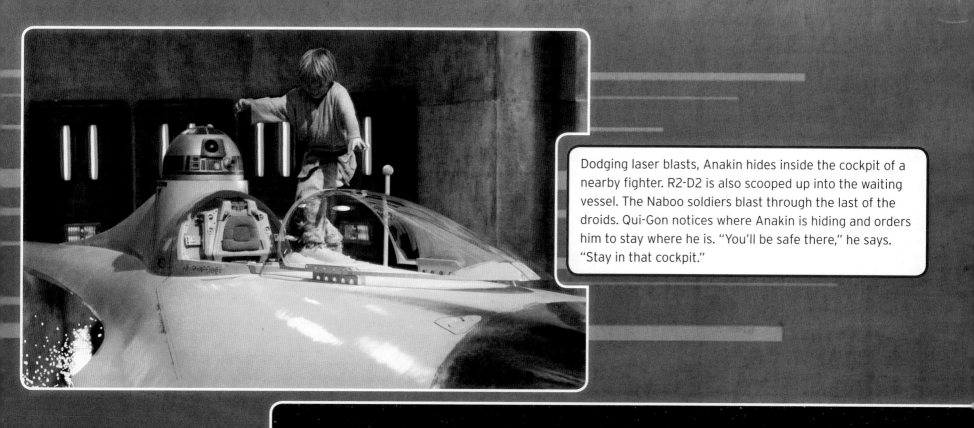

Dodging laser blasts, Anakin hides inside the cockpit of a nearby fighter. R2-D2 is also scooped up into the waiting vessel. The Naboo soldiers blast through the last of the droids. Qui-Gon notices where Anakin is hiding and orders him to stay where he is. "You'll be safe there," he says. "Stay in that cockpit."

High above Naboo, **the massive Droid Control Ship releases swarms of vulture droids into space.** The automated droid starfighters buzz around their mother ship, programmed to protect it.

On the Naboo grasslands, heavy Trade Federation transports fire on the Gungan shield but to no effect. They cease firing. Slowly, the multi-troop transports open their hatches and extend deployment racks packed with droids.

The Gungan soldiers power up their personal shields and ready their catapults and other weapons. Instead of blasters, Gungan use spheres of electric plasma energy called boomers as their weapons.

At a signal from the Droid Control Ship, the battle droids activate and relentlessly march forward. "Ouch time," says a Gungan soldier. The battle droids push through the Gungan shield. Once inside, they open fire. **The ground battle truly begins.**

Jar Jar does his best to command, but he is in way over his head. He grabs a sling loaded with a heavy Gungan boomer and hurls it with all his might. But rather than taking out a droid, he nearly hits his fellow troops.

Inside the hangar bay, the doors leading into the palace slide open. The Queen finds her path blocked by Darth Maul. Qui-Gon recognizes the dark warrior from Tatooine. **"We'll handle this,"** Qui-Gon says confidently. He and Obi-Wan each draw their lightsabers. Maul pulls out his weapon and ignites it at both ends.

Maul's double-bladed weapon slashes toward both of his enemies. Obi-Wan and Qui-Gon parry these swipes, spinning out of reach and forcing Maul to retreat farther into the hangar. Qui-Gon and Obi-Wan work perfectly together, keeping the Sith Lord at bay.

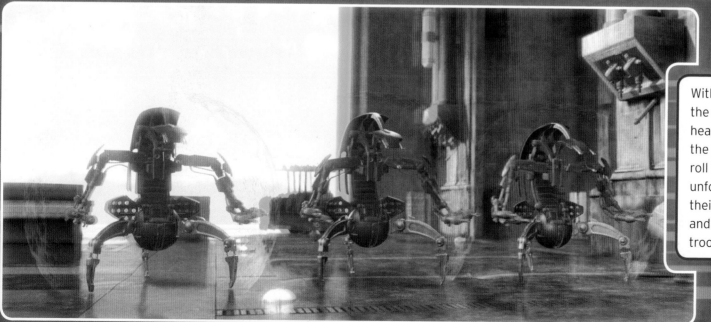

With the lightsaber duel filling the exit, Amidala and her troops head for an alternate path into the palace. But a trio of droidekas roll in from around a corner. They unfold into attack mode, projecting their impenetrable deflector shields and opening fire. Amidala and her troops scramble for cover.

Anakin sees that Padmé is in trouble. **"We've got to do something, Artoo!"** he shouts. Anakin powers up the starship's systems to activate its blasters. "I don't know where the trigger is!" he says, pushing buttons until he finds the fighter's cannon systems. Anakin fires and blows apart the droidekas.

But Anakin cannot stop the starfighter now that he's started it. The fighter's automatic pilot draws it into space. "Try to override it," Anakin tells R2-D2 as he pulls on a flight helmet. The ship flies into the middle of the space battle against the Droid Control Ship. Anakin is eager to try out his piloting skills in a real fight. "Qui-Gon told me to stay in this cockpit, so that's what I'm going to do!" Anakin insists.

The **ferocious lightsaber duel** travels beyond the hangar into an immense power generator lined with catwalks. Maul tries to separate the Jedi. He kicks Obi-Wan off one of the bridge spans, sending him over the edge to a bridge far below.

The plains battle intensifies and becomes a brawl. "Dumb droid! Take that!" Jar Jar shouts. He leaps on a blasted droid, but his feet get tangled in its wiring. Jar Jar tries to free himself. As he stumbles about, the droid's blaster pistol fires haphazardly, taking out more droids.

Once inside the palace, Amidala and her troops escape more battle droids by exiting through a shattered window. Ascension cables are mounted underneath their blaster pistols. They fire them at the roof. The cables reel each of them up several levels, past the battle droids.

In the power generator, Obi-Wan scrambles to his feet after his fall and races to rejoin the fight. The duel brings Darth Maul and Qui-Gon into an inner melting pit chamber, which is guarded by a series of electron ray gates. The deadly gates snap on, momentarily separating the warriors. Qui-Gon takes the moment to collect himself and to meditate on the Force, while **Darth Maul paces like a caged beast**.

On the plains, the droids destroy the Gungan shield generators, exposing the grand army. Jar Jar dives for cover. "Dis is nutsen!" he says. A nearby artillery blast sends him tumbling through the air, and he lands on the cannon barrel of an enemy tank. Another Gungan warrior tosses Jar Jar a small boomer. He uses it to disable the tank, but the droid army has many more tanks.

The Grand Army is soon overwhelmed. **Many Gungan warriors surrender.** "No giben up, General Jar Jar," says a Gungan warrior. "Mesa tink of something."

Jar Jar is surrounded by battle droids. "My give up," he says, throwing his hands in the air. The battle is over.

Inside the palace, Amidala and her guards run toward the throne room. Suddenly, four droidekas roll in, backed up by dozens of battle droids. They are surrounded. "Put down your weapons," Amidala orders bitterly. "They win this round."

High above Naboo, Anakin desperately evades enemy fire. "I'll try spinning!" he says "That's a good trick!" A vulture droid laser bolt clips his ship's wing. **"We're hit, Artoo!"** Anakin yells. The yellow ship spirals out of control, into the hangar bay of the Droid Control Ship.

"I'm trying to stop! I'm trying to stop!" Anakin shouts to Artoo. The Naboo fighter skids to a stop inside the enemy ship. "Everything's overheated," says Anakin. He tries desperately to restart his fighter as security battle droids run toward his ship. **"Oops, this is not good."**

Inside the melting pit, the electron ray gates snap off. Qui-Gon and Darth Maul resume their duel, as Obi-Wan sprints down the corridor to join his Master. The gates power up again, stopping Obi-Wan in his tracks. He watches helplessly as **Maul slices away at Qui-Gon's defenses**. The older Jedi Master grows tired.

Maul pushes his lightsaber handle across Qui-Gon's face, stunning him with the blunt blow. As Qui-Gon stumbles back, Maul spins around and drives his lightsaber through him. *"NOOOOO!"* Obi-Wan shrieks as he watches his Master fall.

When the energy gates open, **Obi-Wan charges Darth Maul**. His blue lightsaber is a blur as he attacks fiercely, forgetting his Jedi teachings. With one swipe, Obi-Wan slices through the handle of Maul's lightsaber, cutting his weapon in two. Maul is left with only a single blade to defend himself.

Darth Maul concentrates his power and sends Obi-Wan reeling with a Force push. Obi-Wan falls backward into the melting pit, but he manages to grab hold of a spout. His lightsaber is not so lucky. Maul kicks it into the pit—where it plummets into nothingness.

Maul grins at his helpless enemy. Obi-Wan centers himself, putting aside his raging emotions. He reaches out with the Force and pulls Qui-Gon's abandoned lightsaber toward him. As it meets his hand, Obi-Wan leaps high into the air, igniting the blade. He lands, and with a slash of his blade, he slices Darth Maul in two. Maul falls backward into the vast pit.

Battle droids march Queen Amidala to the throne room, where she comes face-to-face with Nute Gunray. **"Your little insurrection is at an end, Your Highness,"** he says. Suddenly, another Queen Amidala appears in the doorway. Nute Gunray panics. "After her!" he shouts to his battle droids. "This one's a decoy!"

The battle droids run after the second Queen Amidala. But the first prisoner is the real Queen. She jumps to her throne and opens a secret compartment. Grabbing a pair of blaster pistols, she destroys the remaining droids. **Gunray is surrounded.** "Now, Viceroy, we will discuss a new treaty," Amidala says.

Aboard the Droid Control Ship, the red lights in Anakin's fighter suddenly turn green. "Yes! We have power. Shields up!" Anakin shouts. He begins firing lasers at the incoming droids. Anakin pulls another trigger and launches a pair of torpedoes.

The torpedoes slam into the Droid Control Ship's reactor systems. Explosions begin tearing the huge vessel apart. On the ship's bridge, the Niemoidians tremble in fear. "We're losing power!" a controller reports.

Anakin races through the hangar bay, dodging explosions, droids, and other ships. **"Now this is Podracing!"** he cheers. The flames of the growing explosion lick at his fighter's tail as he escapes the collapsing Droid Control Ship. "Wooo-hooo!"

On the Naboo plains, the battle droids surrounding the Gungans slump over, dropping their guns. "Was'n they doin'?" Jar Jar asks. "They all broke-ed." The Gungans realize **the control ship has been destroyed—the war is over**!

After dispatching Darth Maul, Obi-Wan holds his fallen Master. "Obi-Wan, promise," Qui-Gon whispers with his final breaths. "Promise me you'll train the boy . . . **He is the Chosen One.** He will bring balance . . . train him."

Palpatine and the Jedi Council arrive in Theed. Naboo guards and officials gather to welcome them. Palpatine beams at the crowd, for he is now Supreme Chancellor. He congratulates Queen Amidala on her victory and praises Obi-Wan and Anakin for their bravery. "We will watch your career with great interest," he tells Anakin.

As the sun sets on Theed, Yoda meets with Obi-Wan Kenobi in the palace and confers on him the title of Jedi Knight for his role in defeating the Sith. **The Council also agrees to carry out Qui-Gon's dying wish and grants Obi-Wan permission to train Anakin.**

That night, the Queen, Boss Nass, the Chancellor, many Naboo officials, and several Jedi Council members burn Qui-Gon's body on a pyre and pay their respects to the fallen Jedi.

Anakin cries. He will miss the powerful yet gentle Jedi Master who believed in him. Obi-Wan reveals that the Council has granted him permission to train Anakin. **"You will be a Jedi,"** he tells him.

The avenues of Theed are packed with revelers. **Everyone on Naboo celebrates the victory and freedom.** A Gungan delegation marches down the main street, with proud Gungan soldiers sounding bugles and beating drums.

The parade marches to Queen Amidala. She hands Boss Nass the glowing Globe of Peace—a shimmering symbol of the strengthened friendship between the Naboo and the Gungans. Young Anakin Skywalker smiles. The Padawan is a hero this day, but he knows **his adventures across the galaxy are just beginning**.